Paper Angels

Emma Calder

BLOOMSBURY

LONDON BERLIN NEW YORK

It was the evening before
Christmas Eve, and Nell and
Cory had almost finished
decorating the tree.

'Where's the box
of paper angels?'
asked Cory.

'It's here!'
said Nell.

'Which one shall
we put on top of
the tree this year?'
asked Cory.

But before they could decide, Mum shouted from the kitchen,
'It's supper time and then bed, so you'll have to stop decorating the tree now.'

When everyone was sound asleep,
some whispering voices could be heard . . .

'Well, that year went by fast,'
said Holly.

'I don't agree,
I was cramped
and bored!'
said Ivy.

Paper
Angels

'Who's
going to
be on the top
this year?' wondered Robin.

'It hasn't been me for ages,' sang Carol.

'Or me,' said Snowflake.
'It's annoying having the
children decide by going
eeny, meeny, miny, moe,
so this year we'll choose.'

It wasn't an easy decision.

'It should be me
because I'm the most beautiful.
Look at my eyes,'
sang Carol.

'It should be me because my
dress is the nicest,'
said Snowflake.

'It should be me because
I can balance the best,'
said Robin.

'It has to be me because
I have a lovely, funny face,'
said Holly.

The angels just couldn't agree!

As their squabbling grew louder and louder, they heard a faint cry coming from the box.

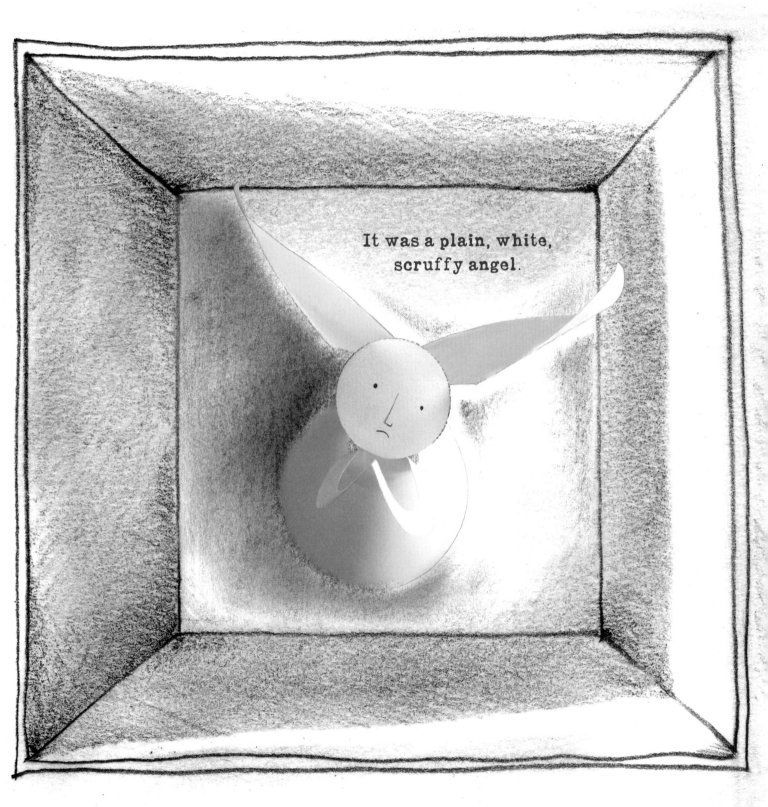

It was a plain, white,
scruffy angel.

'Oh, you poor thing!' cried Holly,
Ivy, Carol and Snowflake as they helped
the last angel out of the box.

'You haven't ever been at the top of the tree, have you?' said Holly.

'Well, I'm not surprised, dressed like that,' laughed Ivy.

'**No,**' cried the angel.

'**Look** at those **poor** little wings. I bet you've never flown,' flapped **Snowflake**.

'And no glitter,' sang **Carol**.

'And with such a plain face,' groaned **Robin**.

'Ooh, there's a lovely
ribbon in here,' said Ivy.

All together, the angels had a great idea and they
immediately became very busy . . .

'I've got some
glue,' said Robin.

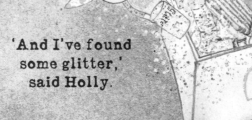

'And I've found
some glitter,'
said Holly.

'Here are some crayons,' sang Carol.

'SSShh,' whispered Snowflake. 'Don't wake the children!'

They set to work. Soon the little angel was transformed
into the most beautiful of them all.

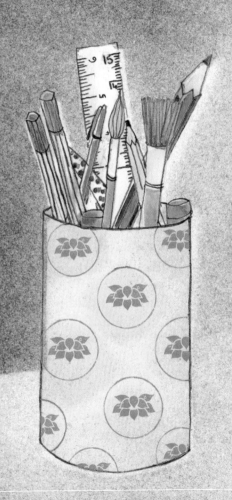

'Do you have a name?'
asked **Snowflake**.

'**Little Star**, of course!'

Holly, Ivy, Robin, Carol and Snowflake
helped Little Star fly to the top of the tree.
Everyone agreed that Little Star was by far
the best angel for the job!

When the family woke up **on Christmas Eve**, they
were all amazed and surprised by the angels **on** the tree,
especially the beautiful angel at the very top.

'The tree is
finished!'
sighed Nell.

'Oh,' cried Cory.
'What shall we
do now?'

I don't
remember
that one.

'Make some
more angels,
of course,' said
Mum, laughing.

Holly

Now you've read the story, make your own angels and decorations to go with them

Before you begin work on the angels, read the instructions on page 31 carefully

If you're very young, ask an adult to help you

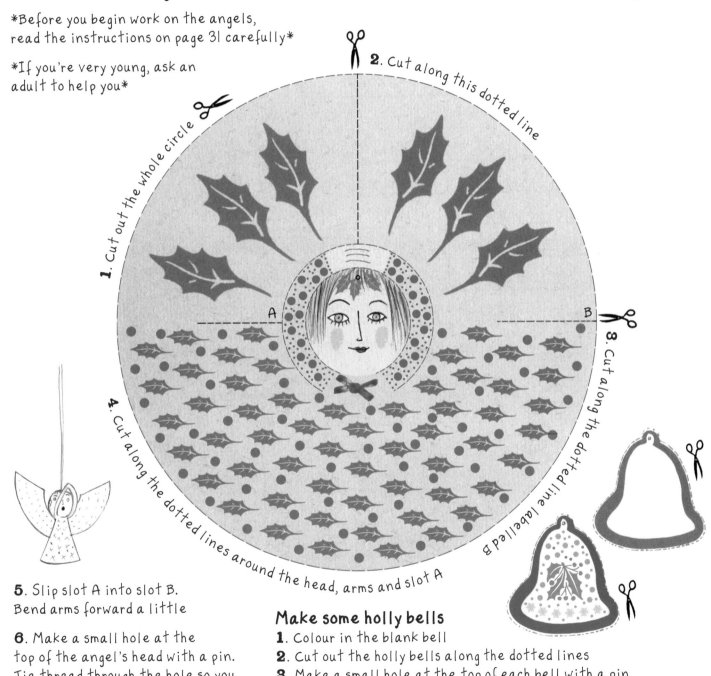

1. Cut out the whole circle

2. Cut along this dotted line

3. Cut along the dotted line labelled B

4. Cut along the dotted lines around the head, arms and slot A

A   B

5. Slip slot A into slot B. Bend arms forward a little

6. Make a small hole at the top of the angel's head with a pin. Tie thread through the hole so you can hang the angel from your tree

Make some holly bells

1. Colour in the blank bell
2. Cut out the holly bells along the dotted lines
3. Make a small hole at the top of each bell with a pin
4. Tie thread through the holes to hang the bells up

Make an ivy spiral

1. Cut out the decoration along the dotted black line
2. Cut along the dotted white line and gently pull out the spiral
3. Make a small hole in the centre of the decoration with a pin
4. Tie thread through the hole so the decoration can hang up

Ivy

2. Cut along this dotted line

1. Cut out the whole circle

3. Cut along the dotted line labelled B

4. Cut along the dotted lines around the head, arms and slot A

A

B

5. Slip slot A into slot B. Bend arms forward a little

6. Make a small hole at the top of the angel's head with a pin. Tie thread through the hole so you can hang the angel from your tree

Make some ivy decorations

1. Colour in the blank decoration
2. Cut out the two decorations along the dotted lines
3. Make a small hole at the top of the decorations with a pin
4. Tie thread through the holes so the decorations can hang up

Make a bird friend for Robin

1. Colour in the bird

2. Cut the bird out along the dotted black lines

3. Insert thread between the wings and glue the bird's body together

4. Fold the wings and tail along the dotted blue lines

5. Your bird is now ready to hang on your tree

Robin

1. Cut out the whole circle

2. Cut along this dotted line

3. Cut along the dotted line labelled B

4. Cut along the dotted lines around the head, arms and slot A

A

B

5. Slip slot A into slot B. Bend arms forward a little

6. Make a small hole at the top of the angel's head with a pin. Tie thread through the hole so you can hang the angel from your tree

Make your own snowflake decorations

1. Colour in the two blank decorations
2. Cut the decorations out along the dotted lines
3. Make a small hole in the top of the decorations with a pin
4. Tie thread through the holes so the decorations can hang up

Snowflake

1. Cut out the whole circle

2. Cut along this dotted line

3. Cut along the dotted line labelled B

4. Cut along the dotted lines around the head, arms and slot A

A

B

5. Slip slot A into slot B. Bend arms forward a little

6. Make a small hole at the top of the angel's head with a pin. Tie thread through the hole so you can hang the angel from your tree

Make a halo for Snowflake

1. Cut the halo out along the dotted line on the halo's edge
2. Cut along the dotted line in the centre of the halo to make a slit for the angel's head to fit in
3. Place the halo on the angel's head

Now make and decorate your own Little Star!

Little Star

Colour in and decorate the angel, then follow
the numbered instructions

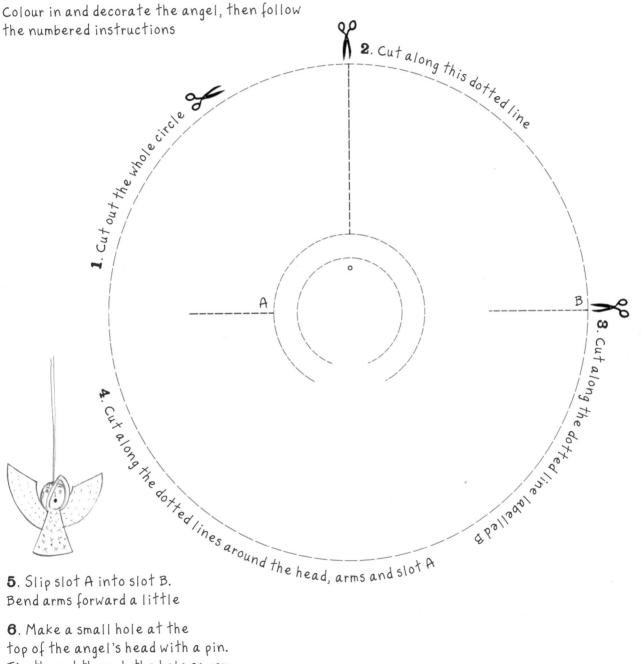

2. Cut along this dotted line

1. Cut out the whole circle

3. Cut along the dotted line labelled B

A

B

4. Cut along the dotted lines around the head, arms and slot A

5. Slip slot A into slot B.
Bend arms forward a little

6. Make a small hole at the
top of the angel's head with a pin.
Tie thread through the hole so you
can hang the angel from your tree